ISBN **978-0-9883533-5-0**

Synz III
(The Wreckoning)

Dedication

For every woman who has ever felt like it was do or die, for my sisters that made to a SAFE HORIZON. This one is for you. You can do it. You are the most beautiful women in the world, because you are still standing strong. If anyone should be able to tell it to you, it should definitely be me.

Chapter 1

As the car pulled up in front the house, Sinclair had to remind her to steady her breaths. Her legs tingled with anticipation. She fought the urge jump and run from the vehicle while it moved. Once she saw the door of the house, it gave her a temporary sense of relief that at least in a moment she wouldn't have to sit next to him any longer.

She could barely wait to get inside and find a private place to read whatever was in the envelope Lori had given her. Synz had already decided that she would take the envelope to the bathroom with her. It was one of the few places that she was sure that she could have a few moments to herself. The car had barely stopped when Synz bolted from the car.

She looked behind as she reached the door. Dan was on her heels. She trembled with eagerness, Synz waited while Dan opened the door. She stepped inside quickly, and nearly knocked Dan to the ground in the process.

"Whoa, what the hell..."Dan yelled.

"Dan, I really have to go to the women's room." Synz said.

"Why didn't you say something in the car?"

Synz didn't respond but instead hastened her pace to the nearest bathroom that was on the first floor. She walked in with her handbag clutched tight, before she slammed and locked the bathroom door. Synz leaned against the cool slab of wood and savored the moment of safety she had felt. The mood was short lived as soon as she touched the clasp on her purse to retrieve the envelope while she made her way to the toilet.

Her hands shook as extracted the pale colored packet from her bag to open it. Synz noticed that there was a small lump inside. She carefully gripped the opposite end to tear open the closure. She ripped opened a slit and removed the contents.

She pulled the folded sheets of paper from inside then saw a small curious device. Synz steadied her nerves and reached for it to inspect it closer. A tiny plastic finger grip covered one end of what appeared to be USB device. She stuffed it in her bra and unfolded the papers.

Synz had just begun to read the letter when she heard Dan turn the bathroom doorknob. She called out that she would be out soon. Her eyes narrowed as she read the words. She had made it to the bottom of the first page when she realized what she had in her hands. Synz folded the envelope and for the time since her ordeal had begun, she had a genuine smile.

Synz refolded the papers and shoved them back into her purse. She flushed the toilet before she turned the water on in the faucet to wash her hands. Synz had been numb inside for weeks. Even with her brief glimmers of hope that had shown up before, they didn't give her the same level of encouragement as the letter had. It would be difficult to for her to cover up her giddiness.

The time had arrived for Dan to discover what his prize truly was. He had been cruel and unnecessarily deviant towards her and others. Synz thought about the women as well. She hadn't intended to sacrifice her so that could go free. When it turned out that way, she was glad that none of them would have to put up with him again.

She missed the days when her biggest worry was Alex's jealousy. Synz had been miffed that Dan had claimed to know everything about her but somehow the obvious fact that she was a lesbian had escaped his attention. To add insult to injury, he persisted in his desires for sex from her. Synz had ridden him into an orgasmic frenzy to save her own ass, but he had never bothered to pay attention to her, past his own needs. Synz had thought about Alex the entire time.

She knew that she hadn't achieved an orgasm because of him. Synz had relied on what she'd felt for Alex so long ago, to make it through. The pool of cum that drenched his loins was real. She had closed her eyes and remembered what it felt like when Alex had gripped her thick cheeks and flew with her on the other side of moon.

There would plenty of time to think of those things later, Synz realized. Now, she had other her own escape on her mind. When she at last opened the bathroom door, Dan stood just a few feet away. Synz shook away the thoughts of Alex as she stepped out.

"What took you so long?" Dan asked.

"Damn, did you time me? It is the bathroom. I don't know how long it's going to be, before I get there. What the rush?" Synz asked.

"No rush, I was just worried that's all."

"About me going potty? What are you into golden showers too? I mean I would happily piss on you. Just let me know. I wouldn't dare deny you the pleasure. I'll hit you with a "Kelly" anytime you'd like Dan."

"That's disgusting Sinclair. I can't believe you said that to me."

"Actually Dan, you're the one that started the inquiry about my potty time. I am going to need for you to mind your own business on a few things."

"Whatever. I was waiting because it is time for you perform your wifely duties. Get in the bedroom. Since you sent the girls away, my needs haven't diminished. Actually, with you around me, it's increased. I'm going to go wash up and I will be there shortly. Be naked, when I arrive."

Synz rolled her eyes at Dan. Again, she contemplated how she to avoid sex with him. She felt that the more she gave in to his demands, the more likely, that she wouldn't be able to draw the line between his will and her own. She grimaced and stomped off towards the stairs.

They had just come back from his mother's funeral, a confrontation by his former mother-in-law, and a family that hated him. It had bothered her that instead of Dan at least being reflective about his day, he wanted sex. Dan wanted to use the prize that he lied and cheated to get. Sinclair had other plans.

She reached the bottom of the stairs and slipped out of her heels just as Dan closed the bathroom door. She turned and ran toward the basement door, quietly opened it, and slid through into the darkness. The basement was dark and quiet. She hoped that what she went to find would be possible in the dark. She feared a light would catch his attention.

Slowly, she made her way down the stairs. The light of day glowed softly like a beacon just over the spot she needed to find through an insignificant window place right above the electrical box. Synz saw the main box to Dan's security system about fifteen feet away from it.

Dan had bragged endlessly about how his money had always afforded the best of everything. His need for "top-notch" everything had been his claim to fame, continued success, and domination of others. He not only maintained but also frequently upgraded his security system. More often than not, he had access to systems that were in the test phase.

Synz heard the water that had begun to flow through the drainpipe from the bath overhead. She sprinted over to the smooth grey box. She saw several USB ports on the side of the box that held flash drives. Several drives were in the box. Synz quickly reasoned that these were backup flash drives that held recorded information from his security, in case his system failed. She reached into her bra and slipped the one she had gotten from the envelope into an empty slot.

Synz felt pressure in her bladder. She hadn't used the bathroom when she went and now in the intensity of the moment, it had begun to pain her from the need to go. She gripped her side and ran back up the stairs. When she made it to the top, she heard the water shut of in the bathroom. Synz scurried past the door and bolted for the stairs.

She reached the bedroom door just as Dan emerged still wet from the bathroom. Synz hunched down, peered through the banister, and looked down at him. He walked around to the kitchen and returned with a bottle, before he turned his sights to the stairs. Synz opened the bedroom door and slid in the room just as he hit the first stair.

"Sinclair, are you ready? I'm so hard for you. I want to break your spine. I feel like sexing you down all-day." Dan said.

Synz stripped out of her clothes from the funeral and flopped across the bed. She balled up and grimaced. The door banged into the wall when Dan slung it open. He frowned when he saw Synz's in a fetal position in the middle of the bed.

Chapter 2

"What the hell is this?" Dan asked.

"I can't have sex with you. I have terrible cramps." Synz said.

"You're not due for another week!"

"Why are you yelling at me? Mr. Know it all, screaming isn't going to make it go away, and all this stress could be the cause. Say one more word and I will scratch your eyeballs out!"

"Huh? Since when do you talk to me like that?"

"Mother nature doesn't give a damn about who you think you are and trust me, right about now I will hurt you and take a nap partner."

Dan stood in the doorway a complete spectacle. Buck naked, and held a bottle of wine, while his semi-hard shaft flopped around aimlessly. He poked his bottom out, as he walked toward the nightstand and slammed the bottle down on it. Synz turned and struggled to keep a smirk in check.

"How do I know you aren't just saying that to keep from having sex with me?" Dan asked.

"What do you want proof? That is disgusting Dan. Why do you think someone always out to do something to you? After all, you haven't done anything wrong here remember? You attempted to use your power and influence to subdue me. What is your problem then? You wanted a woman under your boot. Shut up and take all the things that come with women, which include monthly cycles, cramps, attitudes, and just plain don't feel like it okay? Put some clothes on, I don't want to see that just flap like a deflated balloon in the wind. I'm about to throw up." Synz said.

"But you have to be nice to me and do what I say Sinclair, Will you at least suck it?"

"Oh, you want a blow job? Really? I want to be a signatory on all of those accounts you promised. Put it in your own mouth. I've no idea how my business is doing while I'm up in here and you want your weenie sucked? I married you, you miserable little bastard but my pleasures ain't free."

"You weren't supposed to worry about your petty little business, since I provide for you now…"

"YOU decided my business was petty. I didn't ask you to stalk me or for your opinion. You don't know shit about women, let alone a black woman. Did it ever occur to you that I was reasonably happy? On the other hand, at bare minimum comfortable. You're rich and all you can do with the money is deviant shit. Boy, get out of my face. Stick it in my mouth if you want to and you better have a doctor handy."

"What did you just say to me? Do you know whom you are talking? I will…I will…I will."

"You will do what? Throw me out, divorce me, and return me to that "hovel" of a shack I called home. Go ahead Dan. My business had not failed. You saw me let a woman who wanted to put her face in my behind do so. Yandi probably isn't too happy with you either right now. You had better be careful. Maybe what you think you know and what it is are two different things. Where I'm from, we call you a mark."

"Do you really think I'm going to let you talk me like that, you worthless harlot?"

Synz started to scream at the top of her lungs. Dan eyes widened to nearly the size of plates. She jumped from the bed and wrapped her self in a cover. She continued to scream and wail.

"Stop that. You stop that this instant, Sinclair. I will slap the shit out of you, if you don't stop." Dan said.

Synz jumped up and raced into the hall. She tripped on the cover and fell in a heap. Sinclair balled up and burst out with a scream again. She did so until her throat nearly became raw.

"Very funny Sinclair, nice theatrics." Dan said.

He had followed her from the room. Dan towered over her petite cover wrapped frame and cheered, for a moment. He watched her scoot towards the stairs for minute. Finally, Dan reached down, gripped her by the arms, and dragged, while she kicked and screamed back into the bedroom.

Synz turned her head to where the camera sensor light had blinked briefly to signal it was on record. She flopped and flailed. In his haste, Dan bumped her head on the doorframe. Synz screamed out in pain and gripped her noggin.

Chapter 3

She felt a slight tremor course through her. She imagined that she saw the shadow of a woman, which seemed to float next to him. She believed that she saw ghostly woman's lips move. Synz could not make the words. She didn't know why but almost instinctively, she said the words aloud. It was a poem-like prayer of protection that her mother had taught her back in the first grade.

"Shut your mouth Synz. I'm sick of your nonsense. What is your point anyway? I'm rich, your not. Learn when to close your mouth and do what I say. This will go much smoother for the both of us." Dan said.

Synz went limp as Dan lifted her from the floor and laid her on the bed. She rolled over on her tummy and continued to cry and sob. Her back heaved and contracted in the midst of her convulsions. She noticed that Dan had not said a word to her. At last, Synz lifted her head to see where he was.

Dan had taken a seat at his desk and turned on his computer. He had a webcam pointed directly at her. The large plasma screen showed whole room with her on the bed. Dan masturbated, while he watched her in distress.

"Cut that off Dan. Cut that off right now." Synz yelled.

"No, this is for my collection. If I can't fuck you everyday like I had planned, when I snatched you up, then I'll get something for my troubles. Take the cover and show me your soft skin for the camera Synz. Do it, before I hurt you." Dan said.

"Dan, I did not want to marry you. I just wanted you let to go the girls go and not hurt them. Dan. I'm asking you. I don't want to hurt anyone else, but if I let her out, she will. Just let me go. I don't want to die here. I have a family to get back to, just let me go." Synz wailed.

Dan opened a drawer on the desk. He pulled out a cylindrical vial and flicked the top from it. Synz observed as Dan put the container to his nose and inhaled. His teeth tightened. The structure of his jaw became clear through his skin and he closed his eyes. At last, Dan opened his eyes, tossed the ampule back into the open drawer, and went back to his self-massage on his shaft.

"I'm so powerful that I buy judges favor. Do you really think that anyone give a rats ass about some lowly tramp from the ghetto and her minor business? That slit of yours is out of order but there's nothing wrong with that behind or those lips. I have a mind to run up in there. Take that cover off you and do what I asked of you, now!" Dan said.

"Alex cares, my family cares, all the people you hurt care, all the folks you bullied and lied to care, the people you enslaved care, the people that you ruin their lives care, God does too." Synz whispered.

"What did you say Sinclair? Did you say GOD cares? Did you just say that in MY house? There is no such thing as God. It is a story that was made up to trick dumb people like you into believing whatever you were told. For an intelligent woman that was about the stupidest thing you could have said. Tell me that you do not believe in God Sinclair? Tell me that you don't have "faith" in things you cannot prove! If there is a God, then I suppose I'm the devil then."

"I do. You are a liar. You hide behind your money and pretend that the way you use it is not evil or your fault. You pretend that your lust for dominion over others is okay. You are hiding behind it like a coward. The bad stuff that you did is not okay because you paid someone else to your dirty work. "

"WHERE WAS YOUR GOD WHEN YOU REACHED FOR THAT GUN, SINCLAIR? All he left you was a Bible. That is what he left you, a batch printed words. Most of which you didn't live by, in the first place. You enslaved others too! How stupid are you really? You believe in a God that destroyed Sodom and Gomorrah. He justified my actions towards you then, right?"

"Yes, all he left me was a Bible. I don't know why I wasn't left a way to kill you right off, because I would have. He gave me free will too. I would have not have hesitated to used it to commit murder. Apparently, you have either read or heard some of the stories from it.

They did many other things, prostituted their daughters, gambled in the temple, and had a corrupt law system, unfair taxation, and discrimination, all of which were the law of the land. Therefore, it was widely accepted. He destroyed the place because it was corrupt. If a God who can destroy a whole city wanted to get rid of homosexuals, he could have done so Daniel. Instead, he sent a warning for the people like you to ahead to turn back or suffer.

I need my pajamas. I am not going to strip for you, if you don't like it, handle your business, right here and now. However, I won't run. I'm not afraid of you. The whole world's eyes are on you Daniel. He's coming for you, He's rallying his troops right now, and there is nothing that you can do about it."

"You are quite silly. You think that I believe that. Until this moment, I assumed you were smart, or least, reasonably sane until you said that. You are crazy. No one is watching me, let alone a God that doesn't exist. You rely on your Bible. I will rely on my vast wealth. You have seen what people will choose with their "Free Will". Yes, I believe in "free will". I do whatever I want and nothing and no one can stop…"

"That's what Alister Crowley believed too. That didn't work out for him too well did it? He died strung out, wrinkled and desperate for an heir. Desperate to see a part of him that wasn't always rotten to the core."

Loud drums and horns blared through the mansion from a cracked window. Dan stopped in the middle of his sentence and ran to the window. Synz smiled when she caught the rhythm of the song. She recognized the melody instantly. Dan's forehead wrinkled deeply. His expensive windows vibrated from the waves of sounds came through his house, as if it were made of paper Mache', while he stomped to the window and peered out.

"I wish they wouldn't let them do that. It's quite annoying." Dan moaned.

Synz slid of the bed and she felt as if she glided effortlessly over the floor to a window. Her breath caught in her throat when she looked out the window. Hundreds of children lined up at stand still. The band director's face was familiar from the distance to Synz, the man briefly lifted his head up toward the window, and it appeared to her that he nodded in her direction.

"Yea though, I walk through the valley of the shadow of death. I will no fear evil, for thou art with me. Thy rod and thy staff, they comfort me. Thou prepares a table before in the presence of my enemies, thy anoints my head with oil, my cup runneth over. Surely goodness and mercy shall follow me all the days of my life and I will dwell...." Synz said.

Dan huffed like a raged bull that had prepared to attack a target. She turned and faced him. She heard the band Marshall when he blew his whistle in the distance. Synz prepared her body for Dan's assault. She watched in amazement, as Dan struggled to move towards her, and he appeared to have frozen in position.

Synz didn't know whether it was her imagination or real. Somewhere in the distance over the hundreds of little lights and baby stones that played their music to perfection. Under the watchful eye of the tall, handsome eyes of the Band Director that instructed them through "What Kind of Man?"

She supposed that she heard she heard her one of Uncles say, "I don't give a good hot chocolate. HE got a problem on his hands. He better let her come on home, or she will snap out and tear that house to shreds."

Then the other say, "I got his fake Reverend and some real hot lead in this 45. Dying ain't no way to live, but he gone learn today."

The figure of the large woman on the side that had read from the book waved a handkerchief at them. They both pursed their lips, as if they could see her. When the Director turned on a dime and began to march again with the children in tow, at last Synz could read his jacket.

"Greater is he in me"

Synz walked over to the bed and sat back down. The Band continued to play down the street. She had come to her point that it was time to remind him of who had had chose to bother. She picked up the phone from the nightstand. Dan saw her and leapt from the chair towards her.

She waited until he leaned in to take it from her and swung it. Synz sat on the side of the bed and watched, while Dan fell to the floor and grasped the side of his head. Dan howled in pain as a tiny trickle of blood ran through his fingers. She'd clocked him right in the face.

"I think it would be a good idea to do what I ask Dan. After you are done, I will pack my bags to go on home. Rebuild my clientele, and figure out what else I can branch out into." Synz said.

"You crazy bitch, did you just hit me?" Dan wailed.

"Either that or you're head flew into the phone. I'm not sure if I mentioned it before now but I don't like to be called dirty names. I have a list of options for you. You can stop me whenever I finally come across what works out for you, okay Dan. Let us see Goddess, Ma'am, Mistress, and Miss. However, you can cross bitch, harlot, slut, whore, and whatnot off the list, do you understand?" Synz replied.

"I'm bleeding."

"Yeah, don't do that on the carpet. I have given this a lot of thought. The girls lost their jobs and you didn't give them ANY compensation. It is going to be hard to get new workers since you didn't do right by the last batch. After you clean up, I need you to order a few cars and have them delivered to the girls. I might show you something as soon as that's done."

Dan scowled. He blinked several times while he got up from the floor. Dan stumbled to his feet and steadied him. He wiped the blood away from the end of his eyebrow with the back of his hand. He considered that she had just defended her. Dan huffed and had swollen up and flexed. He showed his clenched teeth to her. Slowly, his chest deflated when observed her response.

Synz cocked her head to the side. She extended her left arm out palm out. Dan swallowed hard when she clasped her long nails into her palm three times. Synz beckoned him to run at her again. However, she still had the phone in her right hand.

Dan went back over to where the computer screen was. He pulled the keyboard closer to him. Synz looked over his shoulder while he opened the internet browser and looked over at her. She folded her arms until he typed in cars into the search engine.

"What kind of cars? I don't know where they went they left here anyway. Can you show me both boobies Synz? I mean the girls are getting cars out this." Dan said.

"Oh, the girls are getting cars, houses, and new jobs." Synz said.

"What do you mean?"

"I'm bringing the girls back into the fold with new positions. Also, find James for me."

"How in the hell am I supposed to do that? I pay people to do this kind of stuff. I don't actually do it."

"Well call your peoples then. Make it happen."

"What are you really up to, Synz?"

"Nothing other than what you asked. If I remember correctly you very clear, "Love me, Sinclair. Love me as you have loved others before me. Now, the girls need some kind of compensation and assurances before I offer them a job. You wanted me to fix this. You lost the women that brought in the clientele. Nobody came to the club because of you."

"You fired them."

"Correction, I let them go. I did not fire anyone. Firing them implies that you were paying them. You were not. All they got was their ass kicked, food, a place to sleep, and had to have sex whenever you said so. That sounds like textbook slavery to me. Maybe you hadn't noticed that I am actually black. Kinky, yes I get that. Slavery? I'm still having some personal issues with the concept. The last thing you want is disgruntled people out there that could help you, but won't because they hate your guts."

"Synz, your plan doesn't make sense to me. How I am supposed to make money by giving them anything? That's going to make my bottom line smaller not bigger."

"Dan, first you need to learn to shut-up some times. The smartest thing you ever did was reach out to me. The way you did it was apprehensible. You owe me. Second, it took Lincoln awhile to figure out that freeing the slaves was smart move for the Union. He didn't get it at first either."

"Lincoln? He was assassinated! That's a crappy example."

"Maybe he took too long thinking about whether to free the slaves or not. I mean he did have a couple of little mixed babies with his mistress first. Maybe it finally dawned on him that if he didn't that in the end it was his own self he was keeping as slave. That it was his own bloodline. You can't win them all, Dan. Besides, once you buy them cars, and houses, you can send them each a nice hefty chunk of change."

"If I pay them, they can say it was prostitution."

"If you send it to them on your own and call it a severance package, you can write it off on your taxes as loss, business expense or something. You wanted me to help you pimp them free. I disagree. Let's call it an executive decision on my part."

"Synz, I don't have to do anything. I blackmailed you remember? I know what you did."

"Really, Dan, while you're at the computer type up this website and take a look."

Synz carefully spelled out the words. She smirked when Dan clicked on the link. It took him to a live feed. Not only was Synz's' business still intact, but one of the men that Dan assumed was dead sat behind a desk.

"NO, he's dead. I'm sure he died. It was in the paper and everything. Okay, you somehow managed to pull a fast one. I'm positive you killed him. I went to his funeral to see if you to showed up." Dan said.

"You mean the one's whose wife told the media that he'd gone on a business trip? When that story came out, you assumed that I'd done it. Call the police smart ass. He had a gambling problem. He spent money gifts for me, on hookers for sex, and the crap tables. You don't think his wife or someone he owed money to had more of a reason to want him dead than I did. Dead men don't send expensive gifts. His wife hadn't left him after all he'd done so you don't in fact know that he's even dead either. You're not the only person with money and connections." Synz said.

"Well, that's irrelevant. I used it to make you marry me. MY plan worked."

"Yeah Dan, you won, yep. Now can you get those severance packages out? I am feeling a little naughty right now and all this talk is squashing the mood. Hurry."

Dan typed with fervor. Synz did her best to keep a straight face while he ordered their cars and paid for them from a corporate account. He reached for his cell phone and made a phone call. Synz listened while Dan told someone on the line to find the girls and deliver the cars before the end of the day.

When he snapped his cell phone shut, Dan quickly leapt up and walked over to the bed. He flopped on the bed and stretched out. He looked over at Synz expectantly. She shook her head no.

"What? I sent them cars like you said." Dan moaned.

"That's only part of what I said. It would be good if you could learn to follow directions Dan." Synz replied.

"I don't like taking orders. I want you to play with it or something. I want sex."

"That's not how this works. You do what I ask; I decide what your reward will be, if any. Depends of how well you do what I asked. You can't lead if you can't follow."

"I'm your husband. You have to do what I say."

"I'm an angry black woman with cramps that doesn't like you. I can kill you right now and there ain't a jury of my peers that will convict nowhere in this country. I said houses, cars, and severance pay."

"Okay, okay, but then we're going to have sex right?"

"Let's see what you come with. I might tie you to this bed and screw your brains out Daniel. I might leave you tied up all day and just screw you to the wall."

"Should I write them checks or send cash?"

"Cash and a note ought to work. Yandi wants to be with her son. Makes sure she has enough to make up for the time you stole from them. She ought to be able to spend some quality time with the boy without having to worry about bills and stuff for quite a while."

"You know, if I hadn't been through so much already to get to you and knew what you're capable of I wouldn't do any of this right? I think you killed those men."

"That would mean that you're attracted to a homicidal female psychopath with sadistic sexual tendencies who happens to be African-American with an incurable addiction to diamonds and stilettos huh? Yeah Dan, I'm the real weirdo here…"

The house phone rang and Synz flinched. She had forgotten she still had it in her hands. She swallowed hard when she felt her heart respond with rapid beats. The second ring seemed louder than the first.

"Are you going to answer that or look it?" Dan asked.

"Here, it's not for me." Synz said.

Chapter 4

Robert Colt arrived at the booth after he had clocked in. As the mail truck approached the security booth, as usual he hit the release button for the traffic arm to raise and allow entrance without any questions. The mail carrier pulled up to the booth and stopped.

"Hey, how are you today?" The mail carrier asked.

"Good, what can I do for you?" Robert replied.

Robert feared a life alone. Women often told him he was cute. Still, deep inside he didn't believe that he would ever have a lover that would accept his desires. He pushed his wants to the back burner and rarely dated. Whenever he did, Robert made sure that there was a cool distance between him and the woman.

While he was usually very generous, it his way to avoid rejection and feel needed. He saw attractiveness as the best way to make himself lovable. He had reasoned that people had to like the good guy persona. More often than not Robert would jump through hoops for a pretty smile and a compliment.

"Listen, I noticed that I've been stuffing mail in Sinclair Welch's mailbox for a while now and every bit of it is still there. Is she out of town, move, or something else that I should know about? I've been on the route for quite a while now, and the one time she went on vacation, she put a hold on her mail and picked it up when she came back. I know you are usually on top of things around here and think you do a wonderful job. Did you notice anything?"

"Not that I know of and now that you mentioned it I haven't seen her. She usually brings her little dog out to walk him around the grounds at least once a day."

"Well her newspapers are stacked up too. So could you check, or whatever you do to make sure everything is all right over there?"

"Sure thing, you said a while huh? I'll look into it and call the apartment manager too."

"Thanks, can you let me know something when I come back through? I'm going to be a while."

"I'm calling right now."

The mail carrier started her truck just as the guard picked up the phone in the booth. He made a call to the apartment manager, who offered no information. He then called main office to find out if perhaps she had left word with another of the security guards, still no information. By the time the mail carrier was done, and returned to the booth, the guard was worried as well.

"I've called in for a relief so I can walk the grounds. I am going to go over and knock on her door. Maybe she's home with the flu or something. I do remember her complaining about some unwanted visitor about two weeks ago. I sure hope everything is all right." The guard said.

A few moments later, another uniformed guard arrived. The first guard shook his hand and briefly explained what the issue was. The mail carrier offered to give the guard a ride over to Sinclair's apartment and he accepted. Two set of eyes were better than one, he reasoned.

The moment that they arrived, this guards' internal instinct told him something was wrong. All of her blinds were closed, except one. While he was not particularly close to any of the residents, he did know a few details about each of them that he had learned over his the time of his employment there. Sinclair for instance, had a small lap dog and many plants near her windows. The closed blinds contradicted the plants main light source, the guard realized.

The mail carrier looked on curiously while Robert knocked on the door. He didn't get a response. If Sinclair was in trouble, it was his job to alert the authorities immediately. He rounded the truck where the mail carrier waited and asked her to drive him around to the back of the complex and she agreed. Robert hopped in and swiftly shut the door, before she pulled off.

Once they arrived to the back door, Robert could feel tightness in his chest. Even from the vehicle, he could see that door wasn't closed properly. His palms became sweaty as he asked the carrier to call the police. He jumped out of the truck and ran towards the door.

By the time he had reached her door, he was out of breath from the run. He pushed the door and it swung open. He yelled out Sinclair's name as he went inside. From the little daylight that shone inside, Robert could see the house was in a state of disorder. He continued to walk through the house and call out for her, while he searched.

When he stepped into the living room, his foot kicked a needle that lay open on the floor. He rationalized that he shouldn't touch it and opted to let the police handle it in case it was evidence of foulness. Robert reached out for the light switch near the stairway that led to the master suite on the second level. He flipped the switch but the light didn't come on.

Still, without the benefit of additional light, he went upstairs and entered her bedroom. His mouth fell open when he saw the condition of her room. Drawers hung open and clothes hung from the side of them. The closet door was ajar and quite a few of her clothes were strewn about the closet floor. Robert tried the light switch in that room too and that light didn't come on either. He then made his way to the bathroom. There was a faint, putrid odor in the air. He yanked back the shower curtain. A clean tub glared back at him.

He ventured back into the bedroom and opened a highboy dresser that stood next to the bathroom door. He gasped when he saw the contents. Several adult toys were jammed into the drawer. A photo album lay on top of the dresser. He picked it up and opened it too.

Robert flipped through the first few pages of the collection. Inside he saw private pictures of Sinclair Welch. Beads of moisture formed on his upper lip. He immediately recognized her from when he had met her at the bar. The woman in the photos was the same woman that had walked out on him.

One of the men, which she had seen at a different place, had referred him to her. She had a house where she entertained only. The man had come by the security booth and as he flipped through a magazine. He had shown the man a cartoon depiction of a dominatrix. The conversation had begun about fantasies and role-play with a woman that dominates. He'd spoke of his interest and the man had given him a number to call.

He recalled that he asked a female guard call for him and pretended she was his assistant. A personal assistant could make it seem as if he was wealthy. Robert had accepted the date and time that she agreed to. He then took the same day off from work for a doctor's appointment.

Robert had requested the appointment because of palpitations. His physician had scheduled him to have a 24-hour Holter monitor test done. A little machine with electrodes on his heart that recorded what his heart did in a day's time. Afterwards, he had confirmed his appointment, kept it, and met her at the bar later on that same day.

When he got there and they met up, it wasn't long before she put her hands on his thigh and nearly caused him to have a heart attack on the spot. He was sure that she had put her hand there to check out his size; instead, she ripped the wire from his chest, told him off, and left. He assumed she didn't want to be blamable for a man with a heart condition. He had been embarrassed; he hadn't bothered to call her again.

He felt a little foolish about it as it were. Those emotions resurfaced as he gazed at the scantily clad pictures of her in full gear. The same woman had passed him several times a month in the booth and he hadn't recognized her. Now, her eyes in the photo convinced him that it was indeed her, although she had appeared very different to him.

The women that he'd seen come through the booth appeared very prim and basic. She wore minimal make-up, dressed very conservative, wore old maid glasses, and spoke as if she was on edge and unsure of her. The version of Sinclair he had seen at the booth was hardly a sex siren, or vixen of any kind, let alone assertive.

In his hands however, the pictures told a very different story. This woman had jet-black hair tousled wildly everywhere. She flaunted her curvy thickness. Her eyes were magnetic and spoke volumes of a thoroughbred, unbridled, pure freak. While her full, pouty lips beckoned one to agree, to whatever they said. She exuded sexual pleasure and the assurance of orgasmic delight. He continued to flip through the pictures. Robert felt his knees weaken a bit after he saw a photo of her crouched over with a woman that sat on the floor with her hand wrapped around her thigh.

"I have to help find her; maybe she will give me another chance." Robert said aloud.

The police arrived in less than five minutes. They listened and took statement from the mail carrier and the guard. One of the officers went to ask the neighbors a few questions and see if they could gather more information. They told guard that they would put out missing persons report based on their suspicions and the length of time it had been since anyone had seen her.

The guard couldn't recalled many visitors or family at her place. The more he had reflected on it, she had just shown up one day, moved in, and kept a low profile. His logic said she had to come from somewhere. He believed that she had a family because she received many gifts and flowers. Perhaps she had gone home to them somewhere.

The police ran caution tape around her the door to mark it off as a potential crime scene. It wasn't long afterwards that the neighbors had begun to come out and ask what was going on. Slowly, Robert was able to gather bits of information that fell into place for him. After he had talked to her nearest neighbor, he finally had a description of a male suspect and the car he had driven.

Exhausted with frustration, Robert went back to booth. He had talked to quite a few people on the way. He hoped he could help find her and that she was safe. He struggled not to think of her in anyway other way. Every time Robert closed his eyes for second, he could clearly see the photographs of her that he had found and it spurred his anxiety.

Chapter 5

Robert sat back in the surveillance booth and sighed. He leaned on the monitors panel and grimaced when his elbow hit a button and begun to rewind footage from earlier in the day. He jumped up and shrieked like a high school girl at a dance. Robert did the Harlem Shake for a second, before he picked up the phone inside the booth and called the main office. Inside the booth, Robert felt his heart leap on the second ring when someone answered. He immediately gave his station, name, and identification number and then asked for a supervisor in the Audio/Visual Department.

"Hello, this is Marcus, how can I help you?" Marcus said.

"Hi there Marcus, this is Robert. I need to ask you a question. What happens to the footage that is in the cameras when the day is over? I had hoped to review some footage from about two weeks ago in relation to a resident's apartment. Something happened with the lights there and her security system inside the house was disabled. We don't know if she left or something happened to her. I have already notified the police. I just hoped that it was some way to see if there was car, visitor, or something that might help?" Robert blurted.

"Sure Robert, I can help. First, the footage is recorded there on site but it is also backed up here at the main office. We duplicate copies and add them to a master reel to keep them in order in the event there is a need to review them. It is a requirement that we have a backup under lock and key. You work for us, so you can come down and review them in the course of an investigation. I think I can get someone out there to cover for you if you would like to do that today. In addition, it doesn't matter if something happened to her the electrical in her security system. It is wired into our system. There are generators underground at each site that we service. They automatically power the security system in the event of a disruption of service from a storm, or blackout that might interfere with security. The footage of whatever happened is transmitted here, recorded, and saved. If the police are still there, would you let them know that for me? Otherwise it will be a few more days before it occurs to them to even contact us."

"I'm on it."

"Oh and Robert? I need you to keep this under your hat. This is information that we only mention on a need to know basis. Since you needed to know, I told you. Now, I have to tell my supervisor and get you another security clearance okay. You might even get a more prestigious assignment after this. You did good work here Robert. I hope they find your missing resident."

"Thank you sir, I appreciate that. I have to go but I'll see you soon."

"Okay then."

Robert almost fell out the booth on the way back to Sinclair's apartment. When he got there, it took a full two minutes for him to catch his breath. The police car was still there with the two officers inside. They awaited the forensic department while they went over their notes. They were startled when Robert caught his breath and begun to pound on the window.

The driver rolled downed the window and frowned.

"Sorry, I know how to find out what happened here. The company I work for...we need to get to corporate right away. It is all on tape...we have it. We have the answers. We are going to find out what happened to her. C'mon, let's go!" Robert said.

"Excuse me? We don't need you to access information in the course of an investigation. The officer said.

"Oh, I see. You want the credit for it. I'm just worried about her. Besides, corporate can send you through all kinds of red tape before you even get to the tapes. You might even need a subpoena. My badge will allow me to walk into corporate and request to view the footage right now with just a signature. I'm required to file a report with them and can get immediate access in order to complete my paperwork, before the end of my shift. Whenever my relief arrives, I will be over at the main office to solve this. Now did you say you would give me a ride over there and accompany me as part of your investigation? That's what I heard anyway."

"I don't like you right now. Hop in back." The driver said.

The officer in the passenger's seat shrugged and nodded over his shoulder. Robert blew a gust of air from his cheeks as he pulled on the car handle and slid in. He usually didn't assert himself. This was important to him. He hoped that if nothing else once they found her, she would be someone he could talk with. More than anything, he really wanted to know that she wasn't in danger. He didn't want to have let harm have come to her on his watch.

He had barely closed the vehicle door when the car sped off. The police officer who drove turned on the sirens much to Robert's delight. Robert smiled in spite of the seriousness of his mission. He leaned back and marveled at the privilege for just a second.

Chapter 6

"I'm with my new bride and I told you I didn't want to be disturbed damn it! I don't care what you want. Don't bother me you moron. Call me again and I will fire you on the spot, do you understand?" Dan yelled into the phone.

"Wow, if you say so." The caller said.

Dan slammed the phone down. He reached up and rubbed the cleft of his neck to massage the stiff muscles in his neck. Dan looked down at Synz on the side of the bed. His shaft dangled exposed dangerously close to her face. He immediately cupped himself and turned from her.

"Who was that Dan?" Synz asked.

"I don't know and I don't care. I'm going to send the girls what I have in my safe for now. I will get one of my people to deliver it today, right now if you want. It will take a day to figure out houses for them though. I need to you to do something to help me relieve this frustration Synz. Get me off or do something to me." Dan said.

"You shouldn't have been rude on the phone because you're upset Dan."

"You are insufferable. I don't think I can't take another minute of you. All you do is criticize, nag, whine, cramp, bitch, moan, and refuse to help with the situation."

"Feel free to throw me out Dan. I see that long list of women lined up to be with you. I forgot how I begged and pleaded with to you want me in the first place. I am starting to think you don't like your prize very much Dan. Other than, have sex with me, and save your sorry ass business, what were your plans? Did you hope that I would fall madly in love with you and we'd live happily ever after?"

"You said it like it could never happen. I mean the sarcasm there was unmistakable. You had plenty of chances to get away from me but you didn't. So yeah, I started to think that you did like me, a little more than what you have admitted. You could adjust to me eventually, if you want. You are my prize. I may have cheated to win you. That doesn't matter now. You even sent your father away so we could be alone. You have to feel something for me."

"Do you not realize that my dad…never mind Dan. You'll find out soon enough."

"You're going to leave me the first chance you get, aren't you Synz? I know I got you the wrong way. I shouldn't have bullied, lied, cheated, or used my money to get to you. It's just that I didn't see how else to…get you notice me."

Synz threw her hand out palm up. Dan closed his lips. She wagged her index finger back and forth. Synz shook her head no as well to emphasize her point.

Dan lowered his head when she got up and came over to him. She gently reached over, cupped Dan's masculine jaw line, and pulled his face up towards hers. Delicately, she stroked his face. He trembled under her touch.

"Excuse me but you caught my attention from across the room. Aside from our obvious differences, I had hoped that you might entertain the idea of a drink, a cool and frosty beverage, hot coffee, whatever suits your fancy, and see if we have anything in common." Synz said.

"Well, I..."Dan said.

"Wait before you shut me down please consider what I said. I am going to write my number down, go over there, and sit down. If you would like to join me, please do. If not, I will understand when you walk out the door. Either way, you have my attention. I will be just over there if you want to continue this conversation. I'll try not to stare and look anxious."

"Damn, you're good at that." Dan said.

Synz went back over to the bed and turned her back to Dan. A few moments later, she cast a shy glance his way. She then turned away and put her hand under her own chin as if deep thought. She tried not to clap, when Dan touched her shoulder.

"Would that have worked with you Sinclair? Really?" Dan asked.

"Did it ever occur to you to approach me like a real man? It seems that you stuck your big nose in my personal business and decided that I would be target to succumb to your power and authority. Did it ever occur to you that if you treated me like a woman that you were interested in as a person, and then I might have responded like one?" Synz replied.

"But you like. I mean you are into and well domination is control and I thought that. See after I saw you through the window."

"It never occurred to you right? It still hadn't occurred to you that even though I obviously don't want to be here, I will do whatever I have to protect what I care about. You went after what you supposed was my weakest spot and latched on like a ruthless pit bull. I am here, but the truth is I have shut you down.

You pulled this crap and yet you cannot make me do, say, or feel anything. You took me out of my element, what did you gain? To make matters worse, I am not going to do a thing to make you feel any better about this. You will have to live with this. If you have any kind of conscience then you are going to continue to sit there and nag yourself.

I don't have to do anything to you Dan. Your question to me just now told me all I need to know about you. You not only believe in something other power and control, you believe in right and wrong. Whether you call it God, or whatever, you know the difference. Even with free will, that people have choices. You're questioning your choice right now Dan."

"Synz, you can't judge me. You beat people within an inch of their lives. You allow them to grovel at your feet, to worship you and your body. You force them to call you names of adoration and refer to you as a Goddess. You're just as guilty as I am."

"Did these people come to me of their own free-will Dan? What did I hold over their head? What did I use to force them? When they wanted to leave, they left. Did I not consider that the pain might become too much and put in a safety measure in the form of a handkerchief, even for your own people? I spoke with my clients at great length Dan. I tried to understand what it was that they wanted and why.

Self-flagellation is an ancient practice. Some people desire to suffer, to feel pain, for some that is the only sensation they can feel. I'm not one of those people. I don't judge you Dan. I simply don't respect you. Your money bought you actors, actresses, and people who feared your wrath. I don't give a damn about you or your money. You are the worst punishment you will ever receive because when this is all said and done, you have to live with yourself.

I will die someday. I'm not afraid. However, my tolerance for a bully is low. A bully is a coward that found someone they think that they can punk. A person who saw a chance to feel superior to someone at last, who took the opportunity to inflict the shame, humiliation, embarrassment, and sense of hopelessness that they once felt. I have more respect for those that refrain from it than take the opportunity.

The horrible thing about a bully is everyone detests them, and they hate themselves. They want respect and admiration. They lack the skills to get it. They can't understand the forces at work in relationships. They don't understand love. That makes it easier for them to resort to the lowest form human behavior. There successes are short lived and often meaningless."

"That enough Sinclair, you don't know me and you don't know anything about me. I'm still in control here."

"Daniel, you were never in control. I know more about you than you think."

"Prove it."

"Ship that money to the girls first."

Dan removed a piece of art from the wall and revealed a safe. He covered the lock with his hand and swiftly entered the combination. When the door opened, he removed several stacks of cash. Dan divided the money into four separate piles on the desk. She watched as he searched the drawers until he found large yellow envelopes. Dan stuffed the money into the wrappers.

Synz rolled her eyes while Dan took a notebook from his desk. He scribbled the addresses on the envelopes from the notebook. Then Dan made a call for his personal courier to come to the house right away. Fifteen minutes later Synz leaned over the upstairs rail while a robe covered Dan passed the envelopes out the door to a courier.

"Deliver the packages, immediately. Charge it to my credit card and add one hundred dollars for the short notice for yourself. Call my cell phone and let me know when it is completed. Better yet, call my wife on the house phone." Dan said.

The man smiled and thanked Dan profusely. Dan slammed the door in his face before he stomped up the stairs. He scowled at Synz when she pointed to the bedroom. Dan listened while the car in his driveway sped off and he went back into the room.

"Okay now prove it. You know so much the tell me." Dan said.

Chapter 7

"Daniel, you are a domineering jerk that seems to be obsessed with control. It has failed so far most likely because of your own insecurities. Your money gave you a way to push your self-doubt back to make way for that overpowering drive for control.

If you could make someone that you admired submit to you, someone like me, then it would be proof to you that the panic you live with daily was silly. You are a user and a leech. You latch on to others around you, identify what you think are their fears and try to exploit them. The way you did with Yandi and her son, Addie and her drinking, me and the photos.

You expected to be able to manipulate whatever power you saw us as having to help you with your own plans, but showed no problem making it personal to get what you wanted. You have shown me that you can be an especially cruel and power-hungry person. I understand that the world can be a harsh place but that is no reason to force your will on others. You don't want me or anyone else to think that you are weak. I know you are weak. You didn't even have the decency to not keep track of the women after they left. Then you stood there and lied about it. Nevertheless, when I put pressure on you to do what I asked, you became withdrawn, moody, and eager to please me. As if that would somehow make us friends.

Whenever you're undisturbed, you use the power you think you have to help others get what they want, but only in exchange for something that you want. I think as a kid, you had someone who loved you very much and someone who bullied that person. You wanted to fight to protect the person that you loved but felt helpless. In the end, you grew to hate the bully in your life. Yet somehow, you have recognized that person as the strong one, and then chose that example over the kind and lovable figure. You are distrustful and most always assume that someone has a negative reason for their actions towards you.

A great deal of that has to do with the fact that you know that you have deliberately put the person in a position to make a choice out of fear. You know that their reaction, their smile, their laughter, should not be genuine, but out of the terror, that you had hoped to stir in them. You built a team of henchmen by means of fright. The first chance they get, they would gladly cut your throat. You put others in a position to get their "hands dirty" on your behalf.

However, you still held them hostage as accomplices in your crimes and then showed no loyalty to them. In your mind, they will not be tempted to tell on you, if they are just as guilty.

Because you are educated and well read, you assume that others should not only respect it but also understand that education makes you superior to them. While it's critically important, it doesn't make you better than an uneducated, nice guy. In short, your education is for you.

You act as if you are too important to be bothered with the little things, like other peoples feelings. You would just as soon let your staff tear each other to shreds, rather than address issues and deal with them. The people around you find you insufferable and annoying. In part, because you have don't have a problem with turning them loose on each other like rabid dogs.

You would make a great leader, if you weren't foul. Your disbelief in religion of any kind is a defense that you have used to justify your behavior. If there is no God, faith, or good will towards each other, then there's no such thing as right, wrong, or morals. I think you believed deeply at one time and had to deal with disappointment.

Daniel, you asked me, where was my God when..., as if somehow you had reached out before and weren't happy with the results. Moreover, you challenged and belittled my personal belief. When I didn't cave, you then tried to point out my "faith" was nonsense for a belief in a God that hated me, according to you.

Your words spoke volumes to me.

Believe in me Synz, I am here in front of you right now. I wield the power. A man and your God has failed you. I can hurt you or protect you. I'm much better than he is. How dare you submit to a concept that you can't prove over me, while I'm standing here?

The need to control others has spilled over to every fiber of your life. Your self-doubt came forward in the form of utter disbelief that I would chose anything other than you. In your mind, the correct answer is whatever you wanted to hear, regardless of whether it was true. You became angry when I didn't respond accordingly. You think people lie to you because you know that you have dealt with them dishonestly. You are in a prison of self-created negative vibes.

The only reason that I'm still here is that you can't understand for the life of you why I haven't broken down. You seem bent on your attempt to mold and groom me into your version of a perfect partner, sexually and otherwise. You pretty much got raped in your own bed and have since begged for more. The difference in between you and I is simple Dan. You have forced your will and attention on others; I made you want my attention. "Synz said.

"Why you arrogant, self-centered, egotistical, self-serving, little…"

"Goddess? Mistress? This is part where you best chose your words carefully. You finally asked me something and I answered you with my opinion. No need to exert your imagined authority over me, I don't believe in it and more importantly, I don't care. Did I touch a nerve there, Dan?"

"I hate you. What the hell are you like a profiler?"

"Oh, I'm offended Daniel. That really cut to the core of my womanhood."

"Someone should tell you about yourself too. You used your body like a weapon. You enjoyed abusing me sexually but you will not admit to it. That would make you look bad and you couldn't pretend to be the victim here. You had an orgasm Synz, and more than one. You have mean streak that you try to hide rather than indulge. That's fake.

You smile when you should cry. Nothing about you is what it seems. You think that you are clever enough to get me to let my defenses down and then you're going to move in for the kill, but I won't let you!"

"See, unlike you Dan, I'm not going to let that slide, because you are way off. You should fire whoever did your investigations because they suck. I didn't pull my vagina on you, you unwrapped it, and yes, it takes a big clit. I didn't enjoy abusing you, I enjoyed the look on your face when you're body betrayed you. I enjoyed causing pleasure.

If stomping your nuts to a floor mat would have caused that same look on your face, I might have done that too, if I was in the mood to enjoy that kind of a moment. I'm not the victim here Dan, you are. The minute I walked up to you in the restaurant, you lost.

You are grieving that loss; I'm merely waiting until you reach the final stage, which is acceptance. Lastly but not least, I did in fact bust a couple. I don't have sex with my clients. I was in a less than desirable situation. I used you for my own selfish needs and pleasure, a few times.

What do you want an apology? Are you going to run and warn the others that I'm on the loose and tell them what I did to you? Sit around the locker room with a few of your henchmen and recount how I took advantage of you repeatedly?"

"Stages of grief? You are a riot. Tell me, do you make this stuff as you go or what?"

"First, is denial? You are having a hard time with this; you supposed it would be okay. Then, came anger. You lashed out at me, Addie, and even the faith of others. Next, you started to bargain, you were willing to do anything to make this right and salvage the situation with money, cars, gifts. Of course afterwards will come the depression, the quiet moments that you stare off into outer space and quit caring.

At last, will come acceptance. The part when you realize that you can't fight this. That your turn to stand the wrath of your own actions is here and you can't hide from it. You are not in control of the world. Everyone isn't afraid of you; your threats and blackmail are meaningless to a woman of all people. I'm more afraid of child birth than you."

The house phone rang again. This time Synz answered it. The courier had made his deliveries. Synz thanked the man and was about to hang up when the line beeped and signaled another call on the line.

Synz clicked over and greeted the caller.

"Hi, could you please tell Dan to cut those damn cameras off! He is all over the internet and the live feed has gone viral on YouTube. I tried to tell him but he cut me off. He's already admitted to several crimes as it is." the Caller screamed.

"Would you calm down and tell me who this is please?" Synz asked.

"Hello Sinclair, you've met me. I'm his attorney. Remember me with papers, he signed, but you didn't? I got a call this morning from someone that mentioned the feed but I thought it was just Daniel and another of his silly publicity stunts. Then someone emailed me the link! I clicked on it and I promise you I can see and hear everything that is going on in that house right now.

He won't listen to me. I'm not defending him for any crimes Sinclair. I'm not a criminal attorney and I had no knowledge of anything he's admitted to. I do recall you crying at the guesthouse though. He's snorting cocaine right now. What is wrong with him? I'm not about to get disbarred for that asshole." Mr. March said.

"I understand. If you will kindly bring those papers by so that I can do my part too, I will come down immediately. I will try to relay the importance of the situation to him and the reason for your call. How long before you can be here?"

"Ten minutes."

"I'll be downstairs and bring my own pen. Since you understand the direction this will probably take, I'm sure you will want those documents in place for when you send your bill for the hours you've worked today. A grand an hour and it seems you have been working on this for while. I understand that you will want that taken care of first thing in the morning after you leave the County building from filing your paperwork."

"Yes Mistress"

"See you in ten then."

Synz slipped on a robe. Daniel turned toward the screen and took another sniff from his vial before he shoved it back in the drawer. Synz shook her head. She told Dan that she had to go down to the door and grab some papers from his lawyer for them to look over. She explained that she realized that he didn't want to be disturbed and that she would handle it.

"Sure" Dan replied.

In his drug-induced haze, Dan absently massaged himself. Synz heard the doorbell and took a pen from Dan's desk. She reasoned that in a few hours everything that wasn't hers would be. She sauntered down the stairs and opened the door for the lawyer.

"I'm not signing a prenuptial agreement." Synz said.

"I didn't even bring it. I just need you sign the papers that give you the authority to sign checks and pay bills." Mr. March said.

"Have you filed the marriage license yet?"

"No, the judge that did the ceremony went on vacation. I have to wait until he gets back and signs them. The papers were drawn up in your maiden name anyway. See, it says Sinclair Welch, not Davies. He must have been high when he called me because I drew up exactly what he told me. He's such a jerk that I was afraid to tell him that he'd made a mistake."

Synz took the documents and skimmed them for where her signature went. She carefully checked the title of each of them to ensure that none of them was prenuptial agreements. After she was done, she signed every one. She shook the attorney's hand and told him it was nice to do business with him.

She closed the door and did a slow grind hip roll before she went back upstairs. Dan had tossed his body across the bed and lay with his genitalia exposed in front of the camera. Synz stood in the doorway and understood this would be a good time to finish him. She thought of that poor little girl he'd thrown out like trash. It would be good to get her some justice.

"Dan, I never wanted to be here." Synz said.

Chapter 8

The police car pulled up to the building on West Grand Street. The Heights Corporate office was a quiet place with little traffic. The pale yellow structure with mirrored windows blended into the row of businesses that lined the street. The officer, who had driven, cut off the sirens, lights, and then the car after he had parked.

The car had just pulled to the curb, when Robert tried to open the door. He immediately realized that he would have to wait until one of the officers opened the door from the outside. He snickered just the same, as he was glad that they had arrived so quickly. Once the officers got out of the car, the driver opened the backseat door.

Robert walked briskly toward the building and disappeared into the front door. When the two officers walked in they were surprised at the state of the art interior. The outside of the building had hidden the expensive surveillance equipment and systems well. Robert spoke to the receptionist and explained the situation briefly.

The receptionist nodded and gave Robert some forms from a tray on her desk for him to complete, while she called Marcus to come up to the desk. Robert had completed the forms and passed them over to her, when Marcus walked into the lobby. The receptionist stamped and recorded the documents, while the men introduced themselves.

Marcus swept his arm out and escorted Robert and the officers to a locked Audio/Visual room. Once they arrived, Marcus punched a twelve-digit code into a panel next to a grey steel door. The men heard a soft click and Marcus swiftly grabbed the handle and pushed the door.

Robert followed Marcus into a room that he'd never known existed. There were computer monitors that lined two adjacent walls. Rows of bookcases and machines lined the two walls that remained. Another door at the farthest end of the room was similar to the one they had just come through. Robert noted that it had an extensive keypad next to it too.

In the center of the floor, two large tables sat with beige metal chairs. On the tables neatly stacked were manuals, legal pads, pens, notepads and three telephones. The tables showed marks of heavy use on the surface but appeared to be sturdy. The room itself was warm, neat, and curiously quiet.

"I called the complex and asked what row her apartment was in, so that I could locate the footage. It turns out there's quite a bit of it, Since we don't have an exact date, we will have to each take a screen and go through the film until we come across something. I started back about six weeks ago." Marcus warned.

"Thank you Marcus. I'm glad they decided to bring me here. I understood it would be much simpler and it turns out, we need each others help after all." Robert said.

The officers looked at each other but remained quiet. They listened as Marcus passed the numbered remotes and explained what they had to do. Each remote controlled a monitor. He had cued two of the monitors already from week one and two. Once they went through footage, if needed he would change the tape to the next tape. The officers and Robert nodded that they all understood the plan.

"I've turned down the volume so we won't get distracted with noise from each others set. I'll cue up two more weeks worth and that way everyone will have a monitor to focus on. Use the remotes to fast forward, rewind, and play. If you find something of interest, you can turn the volume up or down. You can also stop in on details such as a vehicle, person, or area. I can help clear up images on most things. I mean like a face, license plate, or a package. I can't clear up very tiny images, for example what's written on a piece of mail. I would offer you some coffee or snack but liquids aren't allowed in this room. Robert, if don't mind you can help me cue up monitors for you and I. Officers please grab a chair and match your remote number to the monitor number and let's get started, unless you have any other questions." Marcus said.

"Where's the bathroom in case we have to go?" the office that had driven asked.

"Let me know and I'll take you out to it. The same if anyone would like to take a break and get coffee, juice, or snack in the kitchen. I'm the only one with the code that's on site today and you can't get in or out without me." Marcus answered.

Marcus found and cued up more film for him and Robert to view. An hour had passed before Robert stretched his arms. He leaned his head from side to side a few times. Marcus looked over at him, poked Robert in the side, and smiled.

"This lady must have had another way to get in and out. I didn't see her open the door yet in a week. The only thing I have seen is the mail person and a flower truck that she didn't come to the door for." The officer who had been the passenger said.

"Flowers? I remember her being pissed off about some flowers. Can you see the name of the on the side of the truck?" Robert asked.

"No name, but the license plate faces the camera." the officer replied.

Marcus stopped his screen and went over to help zoom in on the vehicles plate. In short order, they were able to read it. The officer put his screen on hold and stood up. He rubbed the back of his thighs before he went over to the tables and picked up a receiver from it cradle. He quickly punched in the phone number to his station. When someone answered, he had given the person his credentials and asked for a read back on a plate number.

The officer looked perplexed while he received the information. His brow wrinkled. The van's plate was registered to a business owned by a local shop. The shop was a short walk from the apartment complex. He thanked the person for the information and hung up. The officer didn't know whether that information was useful or not. He used his own notebook to make a note of it, while he relayed it to his partner. Finally, he went back to view his screen.

Nearly two hours had passed before the men had made it through four weeks of film. Frustration had begun to show on their faces. Most every one of them had a tightness of the jaw line, rubbed their foreheads, or stretched repeatedly. The excitement of a quick answer appeared to begin to fade.

"Robert, I'll cue up some more footage. Is there anything you can think of that might help us figure out what period we should look at?" Marcus asked.

"It's just a hunch but I think we should go a few more weeks back instead of forward. It would probably be a good idea for at least one of us to start on the film from inside her house too." Robert replied.

"When this is over, I'm going to get an application for you to go the Academy. You have definitely got the drive it takes to do this daily." The driver officer said.

"Thanks, I'll really consider that." Robert said.

Marcus cued up three more weeks of film from the outside cameras. It took a while to access the feed from in her home by remote because of the distance. When he did, Sinclair Welch at last came to life on a screen. Marcus cleared his throat as he watched her strip on the way to the bathroom via a recorded tape.

"Umm, it would be nice if you fast forwarded through those parts Marcus." Robert said.

Marcus snickered and pushed the button to forward the tape. The officers both stood up and walked over to the monitor that Marcus and Robert watched. The tape showed Sinclair as she lay down across the bed and fell asleep after her bed. A few hours later, she got up, took a gun from the nightstand, and looked out the blinds. Marcus gasped when he saw the size of the firearm. The officers looked at each other with wide eyes.

"I didn't see a gun in her apartment. We should go back and look for that." Robert said.

The room stayed quiet while the tape played. The men eventually saw her leave the bedroom and reappear downstairs at the kitchen table. Other than a simple, everyday routine, until eventually Sinclair left the apartment. A quiet hush hung in the air.

A few moments after Sinclair left, a man came into her apartment. He was well dressed and seemed to know which way to get to her bedroom easily. He went up the stairs, walked over to her nightstand, and took the gun from it. He picked up a book from the drawer, turned it over a few times, and threw it back in the drawer.

The man then took the gun and threw it under her highboy dresser. He opened her top drawer, removed some of her clothes, and rubbed them. The men watched as the man then searched a basket of used laundry. He rummaged through them until he found a pair of her thongs. He put them to his nose and inhaled deeply.

Sinclair's dog ran from under the bed and clamped down on the man's pants leg. He kicked at the dog, it whimpered, then scrambled back under the bed. The mysterious man then turned and stuffed Sinclair's panties in his pocket. He exited the room, went back down the stairs, and left. The dog then came from under the bed and pulled some of her laundry from the floor under the bed with him protectively.

Marcus continued to let the play until Sinclair came back home. When she returned, Sinclair wasn't alone. The same man was with her. The officers watched while the man closed the blinds. Marcus turned the volume up while everyone in the room watched the exchange between the two on screen.

Robert was visibly on edge after he witnessed the strange man snatch Sinclair by the arm. He grimaced when he saw the man push her to ground and unzip his pants. The officer who had driven had nostrils flared in anger at what he saw after that. Robert turned his head away from the screen as Sinclair ran to the bathroom. The sounds as she expelled the contents of her stomach echoed through the speakers. Robert's eyes had become cloudy.

The men watched as he ordered Sinclair to get her clothes before he swooped in and did near her side. She reeled and collapsed before the unidentified man picked her up and carried her from the apartment. The dog barked frantically and followed the man who carried his owner's limp body. One of the officers put his head down and sighed.

"We need to this to the media right away. There is a chance that someone will know who this person is. Did you see how that pervert manhandled the Mistress? I could strangle him with my bare hands." Robert said.

"Yeah, let's find him and kick him in the privates. What kind of monster treats women like that?" Marcus said.

"Excuse me Robert, I agree we should take this to the media, after we take this footage to station and review it again. I take it you have a few fantasies about Ms. Sinclair?" The passenger officer chuckled.

"This is outrageous! I just want five minutes alone with him before throw you this creep under the slammer!" Robert wailed.

"Oh, he's gonna need to watch his head getting in the back of the car, for real." The driver officer said.

"I will dub this now this, so you can take a copy with you." Marcus said.

A sense of failure wrapped around him, and Robert struggled not to let it show in front of the other men. His face flushed and his cheeks turned crimson. He took short, shallow breaths to remain calm. Robert's expression still showed his internal anguish, while his temple throbbed.

"Robert, we really thank you for your help. I want you be there when we get Sinclair. I'm sorry to tell you, but you can't participate in the investigation once we get to the station. I'd personally love for you to be there though. I'll keep you updated as much as I can. I hope that this time next year, you'll be in this uniform with us. It would be wonderful to have a man like you on the force." The driver officer said.

"I understand. It's official police business. I look forward to that application soon too. That's enough talk guys, please go find Sinclair." Robert said.

Marcus pulled a copy of the tape from a machine on the far wall, labeled it, and then handed it over to the officers. Both he and Robert shook their hands and wished them luck. Robert and Marcus promised to continue to review the footage for clues. Marcus then let the officers out of the building and saw them off.

Chapter 9

Synz stood in the doorway and watched Dan touch and massage himself. He had lost any trace of an erection. She covered her mouth to stifle her laughter. She looked over to the plasma screen and shrugged her shoulders. Synz believed that the drugs had prevented his hard-on.

"Don't stand there and stare at me Synz, get over here and perform your wifely duties. Come over here and satisfy your man." Dan said.

"No. I don't want to." Synz said.

Dan propped up on his elbow and gawked at her. He bared his teeth and growled as he swung his legs off bed. It took less than five seconds to close the distance between him and Synz after he got up. He reached out, grabbed her by the arm, and snatched her into his chest.

"I've humored you today Sinclair. I've listen to your mouth and I've played your little game. Just remember that you don't want me to smack the color off your face and have you just the same but I will. So now, I'm telling you one more time. Get in the bed with me and do what you are supposed to for your husband. I know that you're stubborn and intelligent, but I will break you. You will obey me. You will submit. They always do and you will be no different." Dan said.

"Let my arm go immediately or I will show you exactly how different I am. I've told you that I'm not afraid of you. Your size and strength mean nothing to me. I don't respect you or what you represent. You must not remember that David beat Goliath with a rock." Synz said.

Dan drew his free hand back. Synz held her head up and looked him in the eye. She saw Dan hesitate but she held his scrutiny and didn't flinch. Dan's hand dropped down along with his head.

"Why woman, I sacrificed a rib for you to exist. Why are would you do this to me?" Dan wailed.

Synz pulled her arm away from him and stomped off into the room. She sat in the chair at the desk. He turned and placed his hand on his naked hip but kept his head down. Synz speculated that Dan was genuinely confused at her actions.

"Answer me Synz, why? Don't dance around the question and give me that psychobabble either. Why can't you love me?" Dan asked.

"I don't like you. I don't know you. I don't even want to get to know you. I detest what you represent and what you've done to me, the others, and I don't have your rib. You're not Adam, I'm not Eve. I've warned you, if you put your hands on me again. I will hurt you." Synz said.

"You are a liar and a hypocrite. You enjoy sex as much as the next person but you have been lying to me all morning about your period. I can clearly see there is not as much as a string in your thong. You've denied me, only to annoy me. Even though, I clearly want you. I want you Sinclair, can you understand? I want you to want me too."

"Dan, I'm going to get dressed now. I'm going to put on my clothes and walk out of that door. I need to see a doctor. If you get in my way, I will hurt you. I don't want to hurt anyone that doesn't want pain but I promise you. I will hurt you."

"You are not going anywhere. You will do as you're told."

"I just told you what was about to happen. Accept it."

Synz rose from the chair and went to the closet. She found a simple floral print pullover dress and wriggled into it. She bent over, found a pair of black slip-in shoes, and pushed her slightly swollen feet into them. At last, Synz went to the dresser and found a wood handled hairbrush and tidied up her hair. Finally, Synz walked toward the bedroom door to leave.

Dan grabbed the back of her dress as she attempted to pass him in the doorway. Synz turned on him and immediately grabbed his exposed testicles and dug her nails into them. She twisted them in her hand and glared at Dan as he howled.

When Dan leaned forward to grab her hand, Synz swung and punched him the windpipe as hard as she could. Dan's knees buckled and Synz kneeled down to keep the powerful grip she had on his sac. Tears welled up in Dan's eyes from the pain.

He tried to shove Synz away but when he pushed her, she tightened her grip on his jewels. Dan bent over even more and tried to squirm away from her clutches as he clawed at her hand. Her hand had begun to sting from his attempt to dislodge her from his privates. Dan looked at her just in time to see her swing her leg back.

Synz grabbed Dan's head with her free hand and pushed down. Her finger tips hand begun to go numb. She feared that she might lose her grip at any second. Synz drove her knee into Dan's nose and he hit floor in a daze and tried to cover his nose with his free hand. She used the opportunity and stomped him in the throat twice very swiftly. When Dan gasped for air and clutched his throat, Synz delivered a fierce kick to his exposed scrotum.

Dan screamed. Synz grabbed the door handle and yanked the heavy wood door with all her might. It flew with ease and banged Dan on the side of his head as he clutched his groin. She saw a trickle of blood roll onto the carpet. Synz pushed the door back and yanked it again.

Dan turned his head and tried to scoot back into the room just as she swung the door for the third time. The edge of the door popped Dan in the mouth. She heard the sound of his teeth break, right before he screamed in pure agony. Synz jumped over a bruised and battered Dan, pick up the chair that she had sat in, and then brought it down on his kneecap.

She looked over at the dresser for her next item and saw her in the mirror. Her nostrils flared like an angry bull. Her hair was a disheveled mess. Her chest heaved from the rapid short breaths she took and there were drops of blood on her dress. Synz looked down at Dan on the floor, as he lay broken and bloody.

"I told you not to get in my way." Synz said.

Sinclair ran her fingers through her hair as she stepped over Dan into the hallway. She glanced over her shoulder as she made her way down the stairs. She opened the front door and walked out into the bright sunlight and across the manicured lawn. When she reached the curb, Synz gripped her belly protectively and waved at a car that passed by. A black Mercedes pulled up to her, and a woman rolled down the window.

"What's wrong?" the woman asked.

"Please ma'am, I need to get to a doctor. I just got into a fight." Synz said.

The woman nodded and unlocked her car door. Synz carefully slid into the travelers and buckled up. The driver sped off and took the ramp for the John C. Lodge expressway. She asked Synz several times where she was hurt. She pointed to her swollen and bruised knee. Synz continued to hold her stomach, look out the window, and didn't say a word in response to the woman.

The woman pulled out her cell phone and called the police. She told them what little she knew and then gave directions to the house where she had picked Synz up. She informed the dispatcher that she would take Synz to Receiving Hospital near downtown. A few moments later, the Benz exited the freeway, drove down Martin L. King Blvd to St. Antoine, and swooped into the emergency bay.

Chapter 10

Marcus went back into the archive vault. Robert was back in front of his monitor with a legal pad. He walked over to Robert and put his hand on Robert's shoulder. Robert looked up and shook his head. Marcus went back over to his own monitor and continued to help view the footage from a different angle. Neither main spoke as they went about their task.

It didn't the officers long to reach their destination on from West Grand Corporate office. As soon as they pulled in back, the car radio came on. The dispatcher requested that they check out a Domestic Violence call where the victim was en route to Receiving Hospital. They rolled their eyes at each other. The officer who drove put the car in reverse and pulled back out while the other officer responded to dispatch. They were able get the address of the house where the incident occurred. It was a few blocks from where they were in the Boston Edison district.

As they car pulled up to the house, a man opened the door in a robe. He held his nose and shivered. The officers watched as the he stumbled towards their car. The officer on the passengers' side opened the door and told him to stay there. Dan continued to come at them. He was near blind from the pain. Dan looked up just in time, to see the two officers with guns drawn in his face.

"Whoa, what are the guns for? I got attacked." Dan said.

"I told you to hold it right there sir. Put your hands up where I can see them. I need to check you for weapons, is there anyone else in the house?" The driver asked.

"No, that pyscho attacked me and ran off. I want an arrest made immediately!" Dan said.

The officers were quiet as Dan held his arms out. The officer who drove kept his gun aimed at Dan's forehead whiled the other holstered his gun and approached Dan. He quickly checked Dan for weapons and stepped back. Finally, the officer that drove holstered his weapon too.

"I'm glad that someone called you guys. I will help prosecute fully. I think my nose is broken." Dan moaned.

"Sir, we received a call about a possible Domestic Violence disturbance at this address. We are here to investigate. We need to get some information from you and then we will take your statement." The passenger officer said.

Daniel gave the officer his name, date of birth, and occupation. He watched as the officer took down the information. Dan went into a rage-filled tirade about his injuries. He had begun to shout loudly and the officer asked him three times to calm down before he had finished his story.

"Okay sir, may we have a description of the assailant?" The driver officer asked.

"She's about five foot three, dark skinned, long jet-black hair, very shapely, full lips. Oh, she has the really long, sharp claws for nails and her eyes will mesmerize you." Dan said.

"Excuse me sir, but how tall are you?" The passenger officer asked.

"I'm six foot three, why?" Dan replied.

Dan and the officer heard a howl and heard a loud thump. They both turned and saw the officer who drove on the hood of the City owned vehicle. He had burst out with laughter so hard that he had collapsed on the hood of the car for support. Dan put his head down.

"This is very unprofessional conduct. What is your partners badge number, I'm going to report him." Dan said.

"So your story is that a little whiff of a woman blacked both of your eyes, broke your nose, choked you up, and possibly broke your kneecap, as big as you are? Are you sure that's what you want me to put in this report?" The officer asked.

"There is nothing funny about this. I demand that you do something about it. Yes, it was a woman that attacked me. This isn't an ordinary woman, she into domination and all sorts of kinky stuff! She's vicious and dangerous. I want her locked away for the rest of her life."

"Man, I'm not putting that in my report. This is obviously a lie. You want to tell me the truth because I don't have time for this. Was this kinky sex that went wrong or what? I mean tell me something that makes sense."

"That is what happened!"

The officer who had been on the hood rolled onto the ground as a new wave of laughter hit him. The officer in front of Dan put his hand over his mouth to cover his tooth-filled grin. Dan's eyebrows furrowed together suspiciously, when the officer pretended to cough to hide his giggles. The other officer on the now on the ground sat up, held his side, and then looked over at Dan, before he screamed out in laughter again.

"How did you get back home so quickly?"

"What do you mean? I haven't been anywhere."

Dan folded his arms defiantly and glared at the officer. The officer reviewed his notes again. His smile disappeared as he realized that dispatch had told him the victim was on the way to hospital. The officer decided that Dan wasn't the victim.

"Sir, I need you to turn around and place your hands behind your back."

"For what?"

"Daniel Davies, you are under arrest for Domestic Violence."

Daniel turned away from the officer and began to walk back towards the door of the house. He had only taken a few steps, when he felt the wind knocked from him as he landed on the grass covered ground. His chin caught the brunt of his fall. He passed after his teeth chomped down on the inside of his jaw and filled his mouth with blood.

When Dan came to, he squinted at the bright light. Machines hissed and whirred. He attempted to sit up before he realized that he had been restrained. In addition to the restraints, he had been cuffed to the bed. Dan felt a tear roll down his cheek.

"Can you hear me sir?" A nurse asked.

Daniel tried to his head to follow the sound of the voice he heard. He realized that he couldn't. A stabilizer was on his neck. It rested on his shoulders and cradled the back of his head. It had effectively prevented him from side to side movements of his head.

Then Dan tried to speak. He winced at the incredible pain. He closed his eyes and cried. Dan pursed his lips in disgust.

"I'll go an let the detectives know that your awake. I'll get you some water. You might find it a little hard to talk at first. We had to put a tube in your throat to breathe for you during surgery, so your throat might be sore and dry." The nurse said.

"Okay" Dan whispered.

Dan lay in the hospital bed. A flash of memories flooded his brains. Sinclair in the window, her again on stage, he hands on his chest as she rode him, the deadly gleam in her eyes when she snatched up his family jewels, and then the police when they arrived.

"Hello Daniel, I'm Detective Wilson. I don't know what you can remember but the doctor has told me that he's given you some strong medicine. Before I ask you any questions, I'm going to advise that you are under arrest. You have the right to remain silent. Anything that you say can be used against you in a court of law. You have a right to an attorney. If you cannot afford an attorney, one will be appointed for you. Do you understand these rights, sir?" Detective Wilson asked.

"Yes" Dan croaked.

"Do you want to talk with me, tell me your side of what happened?"

Dan swallowed hard. His mouth was dry and his head had begun to pound. He finally managed to get his throat semi-wet on his own. His thirst was great.

"Water" Dan said.

The Detective walked out and returned with the nurse. She had a pitcher of water and poured Dan a cup. He watched while she filled the cup and placed a straw in it. The nurse reached for the bed control and elevated his head. Dan sucked greedily, when at last she turned towards him with the cup, and leaned the straw into his swollen lips. The detective waited patiently until the nurse took the now empty cup down from Dan's mouth.

"Yes, I understand my rights. What am I charged with?" Dan asked.

"Right now, kidnapping, assault with the intent to great bodily harm, possession of a controlled substance, domestic violence, stalking and resisting arrest." Detective Wilson replied.

"I want a lawyer."

"I'm just interested in your side of the story here Dan. You sure that you don't want to go ahead and tell me your side of things first. You can have a lawyer come in at anytime. I just wanted to get a few facts from you for the record."

"Not without a lawyer, you won't."

"Alright, we'll talk later."

The detective walked to the hospital room door. He shook his head at the two men that waited outside the room. Detective Wilson held the door opened while the nurse left the room first and then followed. He pulled the door up some and spoke in a hushed tone.

"He said he wants a lawyer. Good luck in there." Detective Wilson said.

Dan lay in the bed and stared at the ceiling. He sniffed when snot rolled from his nostrils. He had managed to bring up one hand close enough to wipe away the fluid. When two more men entered the room, he frowned at the mixture of bloody snot that coated his hand. Dan attempted to wipe his hand on the bed sheet.

"Hello Mr. Davies. I'm Country and this is my partner Pagan. We were in the middle of an investigation that concerned a young woman found in a dumpster on one of your properties a few months ago. She'd been badly traumatized and unable to speak. We were wondering if you could tell us anything that could help us." Country said.

"What's the point of sending more police officers in here? I just told the last one to get out?" Dan asked.

"Well Daniel, we aren't police officers. We're just some people you might want to talk with. You know help us out, maybe we can convince the little lady to let the justice system handle you. I think she's on the phone with her parents right now. I hope you can understand that she's upset with you. It might be better for you if you just talk to us man. Besides her man pays us well, I will just as soon put a bullet through your head right now than lose this job." Pagan said.

"Who are you talking about? Her and her man? Do you know who I am?" Dan asked.

"Yeah, a dead man if she cries when she gets on that phone, plain and simple." Country said.

Pagan's cell phone rang. He reached in his suit coat and pulled out his phone. He answered it. He turned to Country and threw his free hand up in the air. Pagan then reached up, gripped the side of his neck, and messaged it. He didn't say a word as he hung of the phone and slipped back in his pocket.

"Who was that?" Country asked.

"Alex" Pagan said.

"It was nice to meet you Dan, enjoy what's left of your life." Country said.

"Was that a threat? The police are outside the door and you are in here making threats on my life?" Dan said.

"If you know like I know, you will call that Detective back in here and beg him to put you in a cell somewhere on an island surrounded by sharks and protected by an army." Pagan said.

"Screw you. You don't scare me." Dan said.

"Fine, but she's Alex's baby. That woman is the core and soul of that fool. There won't even be an investigation when you disappear. Of all the women in the world, why her Dan? It's as if you would have been better off just to put a gun in your mouth and pull the trigger. She is slightly of her rocker, I'll give you that much. Alex is going to watch and encourage her while she brands you with hot irons. Those people don't care about anything but Ms. Lady's happiness." Country said.

"I'm sure I can find jobs for you on my team. What are you making now? I'll double it." Dan said.

"Fuck you and your "team". That girl has the kind of stuff that will drive a person insane and have them refuse the medicine because they like it. We love her. Had they given me the word, I would have blown your brains out already." Country said.

Chapter 11

Synz had been in the emergency room for almost three hours. The doctor had been in and examined her. She'd ordered some tests for Synz and then told her it would be a while before she had results. The doctor had treated the injuries on Synz hands and knee, asked a few more questions, and advised her rest.

She lied back on the cool white sheets and put her hand up across her forehead. The events of the past few weeks had exhausted her. Synz didn't know if she was simply dog-tired or if what she had feared was true. Still, it was possible that she was pregnant. She had lied to Dan. Synz had not had a period since she met him. It was very late.

Synz had planned to get her marriage to Dan resolved quickly. A pregnancy could really complicate the divorce. It could mean that she would be linked to him forever. She didn't seem to be able to fully accept the idea.

Still, the notion of a child of her own wasn't a bad idea to her. She tried to imagine her with a life style very different from the one she had lived so far. The sound of little feet that ran to her and squeals of laughter, soft kisses, nursery rhymes and a reason to bake homemade cookies.

"Oh God, I killed off a cactus from lack of water before." Synz mumbled.

The truth was she didn't know whether she would be happy if she were pregnant. A child would mean she would need to change everything about her life. Clubs, whips, chains, and wild, long nights wasn't her idea of stable childhood. A child would need love, time, and attention. She wasn't sure that she could care for a child.

On the other hand, Synz liked her life before Dan. Synz was most comfortable with her role as a Dominatrix. She didn't have to act a part on stage or at home. What she had indulged in hadn't been forbidden or illegal. She hadn't trampled their choice of freedom, which was important to her.

She had contemplated whether to just accept her alter ego and let that be the end of it. It was her choice to continue the pregnancy or not, if it came to that. The way she gone after Dan earlier, told her something about her. She'd analyzed him, but she fought him fiercely. Once she resolved that she "might" be pregnant, she fought to protect the life that could be in her.

Synz didn't know if that was instinct or attachment. She had only been sure that she wasn't about to let Dan attack her and possibly hurt a baby. It took a tremendous amount of restraint to not to kill him. She responded to the threat she felt when he grabbed her.

Synz pulled the cover up over her from the foot of the bed. She balled up and hugged her belly. She felt the tears as they welled up in her eyes. She sighed and let them go.

She had just begun to relax when she heard someone call her name. She straight up in the bed. Her chest felt as though it would cave in from intense pressure. Anxiety filled her as she awaited the person to come forward and give her the test results.

"Yes" Synz answered.

A man in a suit walked over to her bed. He smiled at her before he patted a spot near her feet. Synz extended her hand and welcomed him to have a seat there. He sat down.

"How are you? I'm Detective Wilson and I know that you've been through a lot but I need to ask you a few questions. Is that okay, are you able to talk with me?" He asked.

"Yeah" Synz said.

"I saw Daniel after I spoke with the other officers who were investigating this case. I had a brief chat with the woman that you flagged down and brought you here. I know you have a very traumatic day Sinclair. First, let me tell you that you are lucky to have made it out of that house alive. I did a little research on the way over here. It seems that women seem to disappear quite a lot around Daniel. Most of them are never to be heard from again."

"Yeah"

"I'm really interested to know what made you fight him back the way you did. I understand that you've been there for quite some time. Did something happen to make you decide to get away or did you just finally have an opportunity?"

"His mother just passed. When we were at the funeral, his former mother-in-law had given me a letter. I had to sneak in the bathroom to read it. When I opened it, there a page of women that had pictures that were reported as missing persons from different states. I supposed it was a sick joke on his mother-n-laws part to have given it to me.

Then, I read the next page. It was handwritten and had the names of women, times, dates, and places where these women had gone with Dan. The dates were very close to the last time that that anyone saw them. Her daughter Lori was one of the women on the flyer. It didn't make sense to me at first."

"What didn't make sense?"

"That Dan would hurt her daughter and continue to tell his ex mother-in-law about other women he'd dated. He seemed to hate her."

"Okay"

"That's when I read further. There was mention of a safety deposit box at the bank with items that belonged to some of the women. The box also contains a life insurance policy for a quarter of a million dollars, of which Dan was the sole beneficiary. Her last will and testament is supposed to be in there with it. The letter was clear that she had paid for the box years in advance. Then it said that she had thrown away the key to it. She wanted the bank to have to alert the police if anyone other than the police tried to get in that box.

She mentioned how she had tried to bring herself to do the right thing long before now. How difficult it was to know what a monster he was. How she'd known when he was a teenager what a ruthless, manipulative, cold-hearted, brutal fiend he was but that she still cared deeply for him. She had tried in the past to get him to accept responsibility for the things that he had done. She even tried to get him help. He continually played the victim in his manipulation.

Inside the envelope was a USB device. The letter said my life would depend on whether the gadget into his security system, which I did. I didn't know what it would do until later when the lawyer called."

"The lawyer called and said what?"

"That everything that was going on in the house was being broadcast across the internet. That the world could see what was going on in a real time feed. Somehow, the device had reversed the flow of information to the outside world."

"What else was in the letter?"

"She wrote that she hoped that Dan finally got the help that he needed while he was locked away for the rest of his life. That she was sorry that she stood by for so long and let him get away with murder. That she felt the guilty for all those women who died before Lori did."

"Do you have the letter?"

"It's at his house."

"Good, I would like to read that for myself. It seems there another mystery involved here. I would love to know why his ex mother-in-law wrote that letter to you. Even more, why she felt guilty about women who died before her daughter did. That just doesn't add up. If this woman has evidence that her son-in-law might be a serial killer then all she had to was call us. To leave him that kind of money is insane."

"She didn't leave him that kind of money. Sir, the woman that wrote that letter knew what kind of greedy bastard he is. He's living high right now but honestly, he has squandered away most of his fortune. He's barely breaking even on a month-to-month basis. That is why wanted me, to revive his business. He needs that money. She was sure he would go after it, she even told him about the policy herself. I think that she felt it would only be a matter of time before he tried to get into the safety deposit box."

"What? You just said Lori's mother gave you the envelope."

"She did give me the envelope, at Dan's mother funeral."

"I thought that's what you said. Her handwriting ought to be enough to prove it."

"Detective Wilson please don't go after Lori's mother, you'd be making a huge mistake."

"What is it about this guy? Oh, c'mon Sinclair, I saw him. You can't say that you fought him like that because you love him. It won't be a mistake; he needs to be off the streets for good."

"Detective, I agree with you."

"Besides, what kind of plan was that? She took the evidence that she does have, locked it in a safety box at a bank, and then threw away the key. Now, I have to get a warrant to get it open."

"Exactly, the box can't be opened without alerting the police. I think the woman that came up with the plan was somewhat brilliant."

"That woman has protected a murderer. She then put in place a system to reward him with a windfall of money."

"Detective Wilson, if you could possibly stop for a minute."

"This angers me. That a woman who claimed to have wanted him thrown in jail for the rest of life, after she paid for an insurance policy that would add quite a bit to his wealth? Which she then put in a safety deposit box along with evidence of his crimes? She would have been better off to wait until her own funeral. The only way any of this would make sense is if..."

"That's what I have been trying to tell you, it was Dan's mother that wrote the letter."

Chapter 12

Synz looked up at the sound of footsteps that gave the impression that someone headed towards them. The steps grew louder and stopped. She clutched her chest. Synz inhaled sharply and held her breath.

It seemed like an eternity before a different doctor walked forward into Synz view. The starch white lab coat said Faith Grain M.D. Dr. Grain spoke to the Detective and asked that he excuse himself. Synz felt her chest deflate as Detective Wilson got up and walked out.

The doctor pulled up a stool and sat down on the bed. She smiled at Synz and introduced herself before she asked Synz to tell her full name and date of birth. Synz gave her the information as she wrung her hands nervously. Dr. Faith reached over and patted Synz's hands gently.

"Sinclair, I came in because I'd like to go over some of the test results that my colleague asked for on you earlier." Dr. Faith said.

"Okay" Synz said.

'One of the tests that we ran is called a total iron binding count or TIBC. The blood test showed that you have an iron deficiency. We generally refer to this as low red blood cells. I need you to understand that iron helps make the red blood cells in your body. The red cells help carry the oxygen through you. With this kind of anemia you might experience bad moods, heavy menstrual cycles, feeling tired for no reason, frequent headaches, and even shortness of breath. Do you understand me so far?"

"Kind of, how did I catch this?"

"You don't catch it Sinclair. A blood condition that is sometimes hereditary. I came in to tell you that we have to run a few more tests to find out what is the cause behind your anemia. It could pregnancy, or that you are losing blood from somewhere that we cannot see easily. It could also be as simple as your body doesn't absorb iron very well, or that you don't eat enough foods that are rich in iron. In the meantime, the nurse will be in to start an IV and from there we will give you some extra iron to increase your red blood cells. Is that okay?"

"Yes"

"Okay then, I'll be back around to check in in while."

"Did they do the pregnancy test?"

"Yes, Sinclair"

"What are the results?"

"Sinclair the results of your pregnancy test are not back yet."

\\

A personal note from the Author

First, I would like to thank you, the reader, for your time and support. I hope that you enjoyed this book and look forward to the opportunity to engage your attention again in the future.

About the Author

Inakat (aka Katina) is a self-published author from Detroit, MI. She is the author of the Synz En Detroit series, along with Smoking Hot Panties I & II. Inakat is a Spoken Word artist, graphics designer, an occasional blogger. She is most comfortable cuddled up with a book.

Connect with me online

@Inakat1 on Twitter

Inakat Publishing on Facebook

www.inakat1.com

www.ingramcontent.com/pod-product-compliance
Lightning Source LLC
Chambersburg PA
CBHW070608180626
46817CB00005B/2042